AFTER BEING STRUCK BY A BOLT OF LIGHTNING AND DOUSED WITH CHEMICALS, POLICE SCIENTIST BARRY ALLEN BECAME THE FASTEST MAN ON EARTH ...

SUPER DC HEROES

The FLASH

WRITTEN BY
SEAN TULIEN

ILLUSTRATED BY
ERIK DOESCHER,
MIKE DeCARLO, AND
LEE LOUGHRIDGE

SHADOW OF THE SUN

www.raintreepublishers.co.uk
Visit our website to find out
more information about
Raintree books.

To order:
☎ Phone 0845 6044371
🖷 Fax +44 (0) 1865 312263
🖳 Email myorders@raintreepublishers.co.uk

Customers from outside the UK please telephone +44 1865 312262

Raintree is an imprint of Capstone Global Library Limited,
a company incorporated in England and Wales having its
registered office at 7 Pilgrim Street, London, EC4V 6LB
– Registered company number: 6695582

First published by Stone Arch Books in 2011
First published in the United Kingdom in 2012
The moral rights of the proprietor have been asserted.

Art Director: Bob Lentz
Designer: Brann Garvey
Production Specialist: Michelle Biedschied
Editor: Vaarunika Dharmapala
Originated by Capstone Global Library Ltd
Printed and bound in China by Leo Paper Products Ltd

ISBN 978 1 406 22714 7 (paperback)
15 14 13 12 11
10 9 8 7 6 5 4 3 2 1

British Library Cataloguing in Publication Data
A full catalogue record for this book is available
from the British Library.

CONTENTS

CHAPTER 1

THE DARKNESS WITHIN

CLINK CLINK CLANK! Warden Gregory Wolfe's truncheon cracked against the bars of the prison cells as he walked past. "Here at Iron Heights Penitentiary, we take pride in keeping the worst criminals locked up," he said. "Whenever the Flash catches a crook, we're ready to hold them."

Senator Michaels eyed the dark, dank prison cells. "The living conditions here are terrible," he said. "Is that why you want more funding for Iron Heights? To improve the quality of life for these men?"

Warden Wolfe came to a halt. Without turning around, he said, "Only a fool would call these monsters *men*." The warden turned, startling the senator. "You see, Senator Michaels, Iron Heights is more than just a simple prison," the warden said, pointing at a large metal door ahead of them. "Through there is the Pipeline. We keep our most dangerous prisoners there."

"Dangerous?" the senator asked.

The warden shrugged and swiped his key card in the magnetic reader next to the door. "See for yourself," he said.

CRRRREEEAAAK! The metal door opened, revealing a corridor draped in shadows. The warden began walking.

"Wait for me!" the senator pleaded, hurrying to catch up.

A moment later, the warden stopped in front of a dark prison cell. "I'd like you to meet someone, Senator," he said.

Senator Michaels turned to look, but saw nothing except metal bars and shadows. "I don't see anything," he said.

Warden Wolfe walked into the dark cell. "Inmate Swift!" he yelled, the veins in his neck bulging. "Step forward!"

An eerie silence swept over the Pipeline like a blanket. A shiver crawled down the senator's spine as he heard the soft scraping of footsteps coming closer.

Suddenly, a strange man stood before them. He wore an old-fashioned suit, complete with a top hat and bow tie.

"*This* is your most dangerous inmate?" the senator scoffed.

"Why, he looks just like Charles Dickens!" the senator added, chuckling.

"It's funny you should say that, my dear Senator," croaked the prisoner. "Charles Dickens is an old friend of mine." A wild grin swept across the man's pale face.

"How can that be possible?" Senator Michaels asked, puzzled. "Charles Dickens died almost 150 years ago!"

"It's quite simple, actually," the prisoner said. "My powers come from the shadows. They give me eternal life, and I am able to shape them as I please." The man glared at Warden Wolfe. "That is, I *was* – until my cane was destroyed."

The strange man suddenly bowed politely to the senator. "Please allow me to properly introduce myself," he purred.

"My name is Richard Swift," the man continued. He raised his eyes to the senator's while remaining bent at the waist. "But my friends call me Shade."

Warden Wolfe interrupted. "Don't let him fool you – he is a dangerous criminal." The warden turned to face the senator, adding proudly, "And Iron Heights is the only thing preventing this monster from terrorizing Central City."

"Watch it, Warden," Shade growled. "I don't appreciate being called names."

"Or you'll do what?" the warden mocked. "You're powerless without your precious cane!"

Shade pointed at a shadowy corner of his cell. "I'll drag you kicking and screaming into the darkness!" he shrieked.

The rage in Shade's voice lingered in the air. The senator and the warden both took a step backwards.

"Ahem," the warden said, composing himself. "So you see, Senator, more funding is essential," he said. "Otherwise, who will keep Central City safe from super-villains caught by the Flash?"

"The Flash?" Shade howled. "*He* is the reason I'm stuck in this filthy hole! *He* is the reason I've lost my powers!"

"Quiet down, Swift!" Warden Wolfe threatened. He reached for his truncheon.

WHOOOOSH! Shadows began to crawl over Shade. Tendrils of darkness wrapped themselves around his body. "What's this?" said the villain, suddenly calm and curious.

A pool of darkness collected beneath his feet. Slowly, Shade slipped into the puddle as if it were quicksand. A wild grin spread across his face as his head slid out of view.

The warden stepped forward nervously, eyeing the empty cell. "Impossible!" he yelled. "Shade's cane was destroyed years ago!"

HAHAHAHA! Senator Michaels heard a sinister laugh coming from beneath him. He clung to the bars of a cell in panic. Just then, he saw something that made him turn as white as a sheet. A mass of shadow rushed towards him! "HELP!" the senator screamed.

The warden turned to see the senator pulled into a swirl of blackness. "What an interesting development!" boomed an unseen voice.

The mass of shade rose up to meet the senator's gaze. A large, toothy grin appeared in the void. "It seems my powers were within me all along," it snarled.

WHOOOOSH! Shadow arms swiftly clutched the senator's arms and legs. They held him face-to-face with the abyss.

"I want to thank you, Senator," Shade said. "I had forgotten how delicious revenge tastes." The villain's black lips opened to reveal a chasm of nothingness.

A blood-curdling scream rang out through the corridors of the prison.

CHAPTER 2

SUNDOWN

A few kilometres away, the orange-red Sun beat down on the streets of Central City. The roads shimmered as heat rose up from the asphalt. A hot spell had hit the city, and the super-heated streets were completely empty. People were hiding in the comfort of their air-conditioned flats and houses.

ZWWWOOOMMMM! A gust of wind sliced through the air as the Flash dashed through Central City at super-speed. Hot on his heels was Kid Flash, his young sidekick.

The two speedsters were racing through the streets as the Flash trained his pupil to become a fully-fledged super hero. The training was difficult. *Hissssss* Drops of sweat sizzled as they struck the street.

ZOOOM! The two speedsters zipped along. Whenever the Flash burst ahead, Kid Flash accelerated to catch up. The young hero chased his mentor up the sides of buildings, through tunnels, and over bridges in a game of super hero tag.

An onlooker would not be able to see the super heroes rush past. But to the speedsters, it was the world that seemed to be flashing by. They saw each other as clear as daylight, despite travelling at the speed of sound.

Suddenly, Kid Flash surged forward and caught up with the Flash. *TAP! TAP!*

"You're it, old man!" Kid Flash joked. As he forked off in another direction, his burst of speed knocked over a postbox. *FLAP!* *FLAP!* *FLAP!* Letters flew everywhere. "Catch me if you can!"

The Flash groaned. *Not again*, he thought. *Bart's being reckless.*

He gathered up the letters, his hands moving faster than the eye could see. The Scarlet Speedster stuffed the envelopes back inside the postbox, turned it upright, and then zoomed after his sidekick.

Kid Flash looked over his shoulder. Flash was close behind. *THWOOOOMMM!!!* Bart suddenly jolted ahead!

Flash pumped his legs and swung his arms faster. He took a deep breath and pushed himself harder than ever before.

But Barry could only watch in surprise as the youth still outran him!

Unknown to Kid Flash, he was approaching the speed of light! CRACKLE! CRACKLE! "What's happening?" he asked. He spun his head up, down, and around, observing the strange glow that now surrounded him. "Is this ... lightning?"

Suddenly, a yell brought Kid Flash back into focus. "BART, STOP!"

SKREEEEEEEECH! Kid Flash put on the brakes. He came to a halt, tearing into the concrete beneath him.

The Flash quickly grabbed both of Bart's shoulders. "Are you all right?" he asked.

Kid Flash shrugged. "Yeah, I'm fine, Barry," he said. "Some strange energy was crawling all over me."

"I don't believe it," Flash said, releasing his grip. He shook his head from side to side. "How is it even possible?"

Kid Flash narrowed his eyes. "How is *what* possible?" he asked.

Flash stared off into the distance, deep in thought. "You just tapped into the Speed Force, Kid," he said.

"'Speed Force'?" Kid Flash said, growing annoyed. "What are you talking about?"

"It's the source of our super-speed," Flash explained. "It powers us."

"You mean, like the Green Lantern's ring?" Kid Flash said, curious. "Or how the yellow Sun gives Superman his strength?"

The Flash shook his head. "No, it's different from that," he replied. "To be honest, I don't really know how it works."

Barry's eyes grew dark and serious. "But what I *do* know," he added, "is that if you don't have perfect control of your superpowers, the Speed Force will consume you – and never let you go."

Kid Flash looked up at his mentor, grinning. "I bet I could escape it."

"Don't get ahead of yourself!" Flash warned. "Take a look at the damage you've already caused today, Bart."

Flash gestured behind them. Newspaper stands were strewn across the empty streets. Rubbish bins hung from trees. Trenches had been dug into the concrete, and they led directly to where Kid Flash was now standing. "Perhaps one day you *will* succeed where the other Speedsters have failed," Flash said. "But first, you have to learn to control your powers."

Kid Flash lifted his head. Anger swept across his face. **ZOOOM!** With the quickness of lightning, he disappeared. He was gone for less than four seconds, but when he returned, everything but the damage to the concrete had been restored!

"Do you still think I'm not ready?" he challenged.

Flash pointed at the trenches in the street. "Some things can't be so easily fixed, Bart," he said. "Perhaps you're not ready to go out on patrol with me after all..."

"What?" said Kid Flash. "Just because of a few stupid footprints –"

Suddenly, Kid Flash's eyes went wide. He noticed that the ground was covered in shadows. The heat from earlier had given way to a cold chill.

When Bart looked up at Barry, he saw him staring into the sky. Kid Flash turned his eyes upwards, following Flash's gaze.

A strange shadow drifted across the horizon. The blazing afternoon Sun was being blanketed by pitch-black darkness.

Kid Flash swallowed hard. "Hey, Barry," Kid Flash said quietly. "Are those clouds … smiling?"

"Those aren't clouds," Flash answered. He stepped between Kid Flash and the creeping shadows. "It's Shade."

CHAPTER 3

SHADOWS THAT MOVE

"Shade?" Kid Flash yelled. "Isn't he locked up at Iron Heights?"

"It seems he's escaped," Flash replied. A long shadow crept within a few centimetres of the Flash's feet. He took a step back. "Let's get to higher ground."

ZWWWOOOOMMMM!

Both speedsters now stood on top of the city's tallest building. From there, they watched the long shadow completely cover the sky.

Only a few lighted windows could be seen in the darkness. Then streetlights flicked on. Kid Flash watched the concrete below. Like frightened creatures, the shadows seemed to back away from the light spilling on to the road. The darkness seemed to be *alive*.

"What are we waiting for, Barry?" asked Kid Flash. He tensed his muscles and clenched his fists. "Let's go after him!"

Flash frowned. "Stay calm, Kid," he said. "Shade isn't some ordinary crook. He's one of the most powerful super-villains alive."

Suddenly, the air shook as a terrible voice rang through the night. "Flash! I'm glad you're here. You shall bear witness as I remake all of Central City in my own dark image!"

Flash tensed up. "Show yourself!" he shouted into the night.

A grey and black eye blinked open in the moving shadows. It hovered above the two super heroes, glaring down at them. Two curled, thin lips parted in the dark void. "Be careful what you wish for," the mouth whispered.

The eye's black pupil spilled down from the sky. *PHWOOT!* A thin line of tar-black fluid dripped down on to the ground, splashing and oozing into a pool of darkness.

The two super heroes stared in disbelief as a top hat slowly emerged from the shadowy muck. Then a pair of glasses came into view. Then a face. Now Richard Swift stood below them!

"As you can see," the villain boasted, "I've learned a few new tricks since we last spoke. You can't possibly defeat me now!"

"We'll see about that!" Kid Flash said. **ZOOOM!** In the blink of an eye, he was standing in front of Shade.

"Where are you, Kid?" Flash yelled from the rooftop, trying to locate his sidekick.

Meanwhile, Kid Flash stood tall in front of Shade on the street below. "You talk too much," Kid Flash said, pointing at the super-villain. "Let's see what you've got!"

"My, aren't you immature," Shade said, trying to provoke the hot-tempered hero. "Who do you think you are, boy?"

"*Boy?*" Kid Flash said angrily. "The name's Kid Flash – and don't you forget it!" He dashed towards Shade at super-speed.

TWANNNGG! Suddenly, a pair of dark hands latched on to Kid Flash's legs, bringing him to a halt.

"How rude," Shade snarled. The shadows beneath his feet began to bubble and pop like boiling, black water. "You need to be taught some manners!"

PHWOOT! Two more limbs shot out from the darkness and held Kid Flash's arms in place. "Let go of me, you creep!" yelled the young super hero.

"Name-calling now?" said Shade, bringing his mouth close to Kid Flash's face. The villain's lips curled open, revealing a perfect, toothy grin. As he chuckled, his warm breath filled Kid Flash's nostrils. "You seem set on speeding things along," Shade said. "So let's cut to the chase!"

Flash heard Bart's yell from below. He rushed to the edge of the building to see Shade raising his top hat into the air. Flash watched in horror as the hat's brim quivered and expanded in size. Shade held it menacingly over Kid Flash's head.

"Because of your mentor, I spent six miserable years in prison," he said, the smile now gone from his face. The hat's brim inched closer to Kid Flash's head. "I think I'll take my revenge on *you*!"

WHOOOOSH! Flash watched as the shadowy hat's edges swirled and churned like a dark vortex. He knew he had only a brief moment to escape.

The Scarlet Speedster sped down the side of the building. **WHAM!** He pushed Kid Flash out of the way.

THUD! Kid Flash hit the ground, landing several metres away. **PHWOOT!** Shadowy arms rose up to hold him down. As he looked up to see what was happening, the lips of the horrible hat wrapped around his mentor. "No!" Kid Flash howled.

The hat closed around the Flash's waist like the mouth of a snake. It had already devoured the top half of his body. Now it was trying to swallow the rest!

FLAP! FLAP! FLAP! The Flash kicked his legs at super-speed, but it was no use. The dark brim inched itself down and around the Scarlet Speedster's legs like a python eating a mouse.

Kid Flash could only watch as the villain's hat swallowed the Scarlet Speedster whole! **MUNCH!**

SNAP! With a click of his fingers, Shade's hat returned to normal size. With a flick of his wrist, the villain tossed his top hat into the air. It twirled three times, then landed on his head. **POP!**

At that moment, Kid Flash was freed from his shadowy shackles. "What did you do with the Flash?" he demanded, jumping to his feet.

"He was a delicious first course," Shade growled. His lips curled into a frown as he turned to face Kid Flash. "But I'm afraid my hunger for revenge has not yet been satisfied."

The brim of his hat begin to ripple as he once again lifted it off his head...

CHAPTER 4

THE DEAD OF NIGHT

Kid Flash watched as the hat moved towards him. This man had just defeated his mentor. That fact frightened him ... but it also made him angry! **ZOOOM!** Kid Flash smashed into the villain at super-speed. **SLAM!**

"Urk!" Shade flew forwards and landed in a heap. Groggily, he raised himself up. His eyes shot back at Kid Flash. "I'll have your head for that!"

BOOM! A sudden burst of intense light lit up the scene!

The Flash, shadows wrapped around his legs like claws, emerged from the darkness. The energy from the Flash's super-speed had driven off Shade's shadows for a moment. However, the Flash's body was still wrapped in a dark cocoon. His hands gripped the ground desperately as the shadow arms strained to pull the rest of his body back into the darkness.

"You're alive!" Kid Flash shouted. He reached out his hand.

The shadow arms jerked at the Flash. Black tentacles wrapped around the super hero's neck. "Don't come any closer!" he yelled at Kid Flash. "Run!"

"No!" the hero said. "I won't leave you!"

Flash groaned and clenched his fingers tighter. His grip was slipping.

"You have to!" Flash said. "His hold on me is too strong, I –" Swirling shadows wrapped around Flash's mouth, silencing him. His fingers dragged along the ground as the darkness pulled him deeper and deeper into the shadows. Soon, only his eyes remained visible.

Kid Flash burst at super-speed towards the Flash, but there was nothing to grab. "No!" Kid Flash howled. *SPLASH!* His hands dug through the inky shadows, but his fists found nothing but darkness. The Flash was gone.

PHWOOT! Now Shade stood in front of Kid Flash. He cleared his throat and straightened his bow tie. "Please pardon the interruption," Shade said.

Shade leaned towards the young hero threateningly. "Now, where were we...?"

Shadows bled out from Shade's footsteps in all directions. They transformed into sharp-looking knives and blades.

"No more games," Shade said. A crooked smile danced across his face. He raised his hands in a threatening gesture, and the shadow weapons surrounded Kid Flash, hovering just centimetres above the young speedster. "Let's see you run your way out of this!"

Kid Flash's face lit up. "Be careful what you wish for," Kid Flash said. He suddenly burst into super-speed!

Bart began to run sharp circles around the super-villain. "This again?" Shade said, unimpressed, as wind surrounded him and his weapons. But Kid Flash did not listen.

The edges of the Shade's shadowy weapons began to blur. Bart kept running. Mental images flew through his mind. *Central City draped in darkness.* Bart ran faster. *The Flash, imprisoned in a world of shadows.* He increased his speed again. Bart kept speeding up, but he remained in control of himself.

The vortex of wind tossed Shade left and right like a rag doll caught in a hurricane. "Clever boy," the villain shouted. "But it's not nearly enough!" He began to wrap his shadows around him in a protective shield.

Kid Flash knew that Shade was trying to teleport away to safety. Then the villain would reappear elsewhere and continue his attack. A feeling of desperation began to crawl over Bart.

Kid Flash was frightened.

ZOOOM! The fear just made Bart run faster! Suddenly, a familiar tingling sensation ran through Kid Flash's body. He felt as light as air, and as quick as greased lightning. *CRACKLE!* Yellow energy burst from the speedster's body.

Fingers of shadow wrapped themselves around Shade's head. Kid Flash saw that the villain was about to free himself.

It's now or never, Kid Flash thought.

CHAPTER 5

DAWN OF A NEW DAY

ZHHINNGG!! Yellow lightning surrounded the scene. The blinding burst of light erased all hints of shadow on the streets. **CRACKLE! CRACKLE!** The ball of light exploded further outwards! Soon the entire city was illuminated.

When the light faded, the Sun once again shone its orange-red rays on the city. The blast had sliced through the city's dark prison, as well as the shadowy shield Shade had wrapped around himself. The villain slumped in a heap upon the concrete.

On the ground next to him lay the Flash. He had been freed from his dark prison. "Nice work, Bart!" Flash said, getting to his feet. "I don't know how you did it, but I'm glad you did."

Flash looked left and right, but Kid Flash was nowhere to be seen. The Scarlet Speedster ran back and forth searching frantically for the young hero "Bart, where are you?" he yelled. "BART?"

CRAAAAACK!! A burst of light flared up, creating a slit in the air just in front of Flash. "What the –?"

The slit lengthened, and then widened into a gap. **BANG! BOOM! CRACKLE!** Yellow lightning exploded out on to the ground, brightening everything. Flash shielded his eyes against the intense light. "The Speed Force!" he shouted. "But how?"

Just then, a red-gloved hand emerged from the gap. It reached out towards Flash. Barry heard a whisper ring through his mind. It said, as clear as day, *Help me!*

Flash stepped forward and grabbed the hand. He pulled with all his might. Bit by bit, the hand grew into a shoulder. Flash pulled harder still, and a face emerged – the face of Kid Flash! "Hold on, Bart!"

Flash pumped his legs at super-speed. **THUD! THUD! THUD!** His feet slammed against the concrete, wearing it down with the repeated motion. "Fight it, Kid!" Barry yelled. "I believe in you!"

Suddenly, Bart burst free! **WHAM!** The two speedsters landed in a heap. They both looked up at the glowing crack above them as it narrowed quickly into a seam. Then, with a **POP!** – it disappeared!

Barry stood and held out his hand to Bart. "Glad to have you back, Kid," he said.

Kid Flash smiled. "Thanks."

"I wish I could've seen it," Flash said.

"The Speed Force?" Kid Flash asked.

"No," Flash answered, chuckling. "The look on Shade's face when you beat him!"

Bart laughed. He looked at the unconscious super-villain at their feet. "So what are we going to do with him?" Kid Flash asked, poking him with his foot. "We can't lock him back up at Iron Heights – not anymore."

"True," Flash said, grinning. "But I think I can shed some *light* on the subject."

Kid Flash rolled his eyes at the Flash's bad pun. "Give me a break, Barry."

*　　*　　*

Later, at a secret laboratory, the two speedsters stood in front of a brilliant light source. They had secured one thousand mega-watt light bulbs on to the walls of a square room. Until Iron Heights Penitentiary could build a similar holding cell, Shade would remain their prisoner, powerless inside the makeshift light box.

"Tell me," Flash said, "how did you manage to escape the Speed Force?"

"Honestly?" replied Kid Flash. "I thought about what you said earlier. About controlling my superpowers. I thought about the city, and what would happen to it if I failed." Kid Flash paused. "And I thought about you," he added. "You were right – I'm not ready to do this super hero stuff." He looked down at his feet.

"Actually," Flash said, smiling proudly, "I think you proved yourself today."

Kid Flash beamed up at his mentor. "Really?" he asked, excited. "Does that mean I can I go on patrol with you now?"

"Yep," Flash said proudly. "I mean, we both know you have a temper..."

A hint of anger crossed Kid's face – but it faded almost as quickly. "Yeah," he said. "I know."

Flash put a hand on Bart's shoulder. "We all have some darkness inside us," Flash admitted.

Kid Flash nodded. He pointed at the cell in front of them. "I guess what matters is that we don't let our dark sides control us."

Flash grinned. "I always knew you were a *bright* kid."

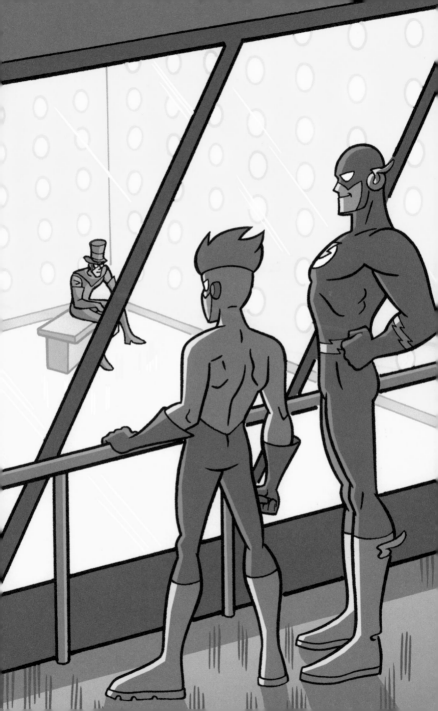

SHADE

REAL NAME: RICHARD SWIFT

OCCUPATION: PROFESSIONAL CRIMINAL

HEIGHT: 1.88 METRES

WEIGHT: 77 KILOGRAMS

EYES: BLACK

HAIR: BLACK

SPECIAL POWERS/ABILITIES:

Can control shadows and use them as weapons or prisons; shadow teleportation; limited invulnerability; long life.

done

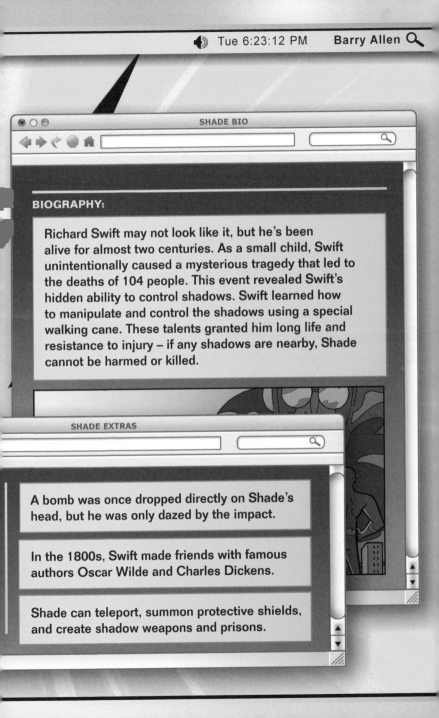

SHADE BIO

BIOGRAPHY:

Richard Swift may not look like it, but he's been alive for almost two centuries. As a small child, Swift unintentionally caused a mysterious tragedy that led to the deaths of 104 people. This event revealed Swift's hidden ability to control shadows. Swift learned how to manipulate and control the shadows using a special walking cane. These talents granted him long life and resistance to injury – if any shadows are nearby, Shade cannot be harmed or killed.

SHADE EXTRAS

A bomb was once dropped directly on Shade's head, but he was only dazed by the impact.

In the 1800s, Swift made friends with famous authors Oscar Wilde and Charles Dickens.

Shade can teleport, summon protective shields, and create shadow weapons and prisons.

BIOGRAPHIES

Sean Tulien is a children's book editor. In his spare time, he likes to read comic books, eat sushi, exercise outdoors, go for long walks at night, listen to loud music, and write books like this one.

Erik Doescher is a freelance illustrator. He worked for a number of comic studios throughout the 1990s, and then moved into videogame development and design. However, he has not given up on illustrating his favourite comic book characters.

Mike DeCarlo is a long-term contributor of comic art whose range extends from Batman and Iron Man to Bugs Bunny and Scooby-Doo. He lives with his wife and four children.

Lee Loughridge has been working in comics for more than fifteen years. He currently lives in a tent on the beach.

GLOSSARY

abyss very deep hole that seems to have no bottom

chasm deep crack

illuminate light something up very brightly

mentor wise and trusted teacher

provoke to deliberately annoy or anger someone

pun joke that makes use of different meanings of the same word

scoff to ridicule or dismiss someone

sinister evil and threatening

Speed Force dimension of energy that gives speedsters, like the Flash and Kid Flash, their superpowers

teleport transport someone or something across space and distance instantly

void empty space

vortex spinning, whirling mass

DISCUSSION QUESTIONS

1. Whose superpowers do you think are cooler – Flash's super-speed, or Shade's shadow powers? Why?

2. Kid Flash and Flash help each other to protect Central City. If you were a super hero, who would your sidekick be?

3. Which illustration in this book was your favourite? Why?

WRITING PROMPTS

1. Shade can teleport through shadows to go anywhere he wants. If you could do the same, where would you go? What would you do? Write about your life.

2. The shadowy Shade has returned – and you have the power of light! How will you use your command of light to overcome the dark Shade? Write about your epic battle.

3. Think up your own super hero or super-villain. What talents does he or she have? What does his or her costume look like? Does he or she have any weaknesses? Write about your character, then draw a picture!

MORE NEW The FLASH ADVENTURES!

WRATH OF THE
WEATHER WIZARD

ATTACK OF
PROFESSOR ZOOM!

SHELL SHOCKER

CAPTAIN COLD'S
ARCTIC ERUPTION

GORILLA WARFARE